ELSIE O. DENNIS
AUTHOR OF TWILIGHT AT DAWN

I0557873

GOD
IS NOT
HERE

SOPHOS
SB
BOOKS

God is Not Here
Copyright © 2017 Elsie O. Dennis

Published in Nigeria by
ElsieWrite Ltd.
FCT Abuja, Nigeria.
elsiewrite@gmail.com

International edition published by
Sophos Books Ltd.
Croydon
publishwithsophos@gmail.com

ISBN 978-1-905669-36-3

Cover design by Busayo Lawrence
Printed in the United Kingdom

To the memory of Astro, the brave one,
my hero in uniform who first showed me what true
courage looks like. May you continue to rest in peace.

To the memories of my father and mother,
who saw the decimation of the Niger Delta up close
but were powerless to do anything about it.

And to the countless young men and women,
who die daily in various ways
in the creeks of the Niger Delta.

The Niger Delta

The Delta region of Nigeria is an interesting place. A land of tropical rainforests, great rivers and abundant natural resources. The region is home to some of the most sought-after cash crops in the world; crops like rubber, palm oil, coconut and cassava and bamboo are just a few of the crops in this region. It is also home to some of Africa's hardiest people, a melting pot of people with distinct yet, similar traditions and a unique way of life. The people of this region are strong, resilient, fearless and intelligent. To the outsider, they come across as aggressive and loud, but this is not necessarily so. They are a boisterous people with a happy-go-lucky attitude to life.

In 1959, crude oil was discovered in Oloibiri in Rivers state. It was soon realised that this oil was not only of very high quality but was also available in huge commercial quantity. Overnight, the region became a

Mecca of sorts for oil exploration companies and government interests. Nigeria had found her cash cow and the future looked bright. Unfortunately, when the money started flowing, the cow was ignored. A complex mix of greed, avarice and corruption plunged the region into deeper mess and while the oil money funded developments in other parts of the country and paid for everything the country needed, the Niger Delta was left underdeveloped.

The frustration and agitation of the people soon resulted in militancy. Various governments have tried different palliatives, but the largely uneducated youths have found an easy outlet for their frustrations in kidnapping, thuggery and senseless violence. The oil exploration firms have taken advantage of the greed of the community leaders to do as little as they can get away with for the host communities. On the other hand, the community leaders corruptly enriched themselves with the resources meant for their people. The result was a monster that no one could tame.

This story, although a complete work of fiction, attempts to draw some parallel between events in the region and current realities.

Enjoy!

Elsie O. Dennis

Prologue

Somewhere in the nation's capital…

The director was feeling totally frustrated as he walked into his office. He knew disaster lay ahead but he had no way of averting it. He had exhausted every argument he had with the military top brass, but no one was willing to listen. He locked his office door behind him. He did not want to be disturbed, he needed to think. Even though it was near close of work some overzealous staff could still come in to say the usual inanities they were used to just to be sure they were noticed. He was not in the mood today for any of that. In fact, he was not in the mood for anything that resembled sycophancy of any sort. He had had enough of it already today. He had just been called a sycophant and he was still smarting from the shame of it.

He sank into his plush office sofa and allowed his mind to drift back to the meeting he had just walked away from.

"With all due respect sir, I think we should wait until we have better info before sending the team to Yemowei. I believe it is foolhardy to send them in based on of the scanty information we have. Those militant boys are more sophisticated than we give them credit for. It will not surprise me if they already know how strategic the town is. In which case our boys would be walking into a trap!"

"Dr. Agbai, I have a problem with you book people" the General looked around at his officers around the table as he spoke, he noticed they were enjoying his speech and he took a sip of water from the glass in front of him as he continued. Everyone else had a soft drink or tea or coffee but not the general. It was rumoured that he only drank water, and no one had ever seen him drink anything else in public.

"To begin with, I know that whenever anyone starts a statement with all due respect, the intention is to insult. I take an exception to your opinion that we are sending in our team carelessly. Whatever information is available to those rascals at this point can only have come from this room. No one outside of here is supposed to know what we are up to.

Besides the team we are sending is a well-trained elite team. Their leader is the best we have in his category and we have spared no expense in their training. So, whoever is planning to send information to the local rascals should tell them to prepare to be exterminated like the vermin they are!"

The General had not raised his voice at all, but it was clear he was dead serious. His even tone of voice sent chills down the spine of his listeners, and some of the officers were noticeably fidgeting. Dr. Agbai was uncomfortable where he sat but his discomfort was heightened by his inability to make the general see reason. He was more familiar with the Niger Delta than any other person in the room, which was why he had been called in to the meeting in the first place, but it was clear they were through with him, and his opinion was not needed any further. He had a deep sense of foreboding but there was nothing more he could say or do. He sent up a silent prayer on behalf of the soldiers that would be going to the creeks of the Delta. And he prayed he was wrong.

1

"I'm feeling very cold, please cover me up," Alero pleaded in a trembling voice. The two men closest to her exchanged worried glances. She was shaking violently, and it was clear she was in a bad way. Her body was burning up and they had been sponging her almost nonstop for the past two hours. The fever did not seem to be abating at all. They had used up the last of the balm they had on her without any apparent relief.

"Maybe we should go outside for a bit of fresh air," Gbaja suggested worriedly. The leader glanced at him without comment.

"Gbaja you must be joking!" Alero hissed weakly. "Go outside to where?"

It was clear the young man was no longer thinking coherently. There was no going outside this night or indeed anytime soon.

Their days of going outside had ended abruptly a few days before when they had heard movement and the distant sound of a whistle had told them in no uncertain terms that their little hide out was in danger of discovery. Luckily the sounds had started long after the "boss" had come back in from foraging for herbs to bring down Alero's fever.

She had suddenly grown worse since that night three days ago and the herbs had seemed useless. They had been boiling them for her to drink but since then had been too afraid to light a fire for fear of being found out. They had been forced to chew on dry biscuits and warm up a little water with a cigarette lighter for Alero.

It was a pretty miserable existence at the moment, but it was the girl's fever that had the little band of fugitives worried till they were almost sick themselves. All, that is, except for one.

Timmy appeared totally unmoved and kept reassuring them that the girl would be alright, and they had nothing to worry about. He had left them alone several hours ago after laying his big yet gentle hands on the girl and praying fervently. He had retreated to his corner and had been in what appeared to be in an agony ever since. They knew better than to disturb him when he was like that. In fact, he usually appeared not able to hear and they had learned to leave him alone after the last incident when they had almost incinerated themselves...

They left Timmy well alone and focused on the girl who seemed to be slipping away from them. They were afraid she could begin to convulse if the fever did not break soon.

"I feel very feverish and uncomfortable."

Alero complained for the umpteenth time. The fever was clearly getting worse, they could almost see her slipping away from them as they watched helplessly and all their feeble attempts to bring down the fever had so far failed. The situation was getting out of hand, and the men were at breaking point.

"Maybe we should risk it and go for a walk to help clear your head a little bit."

Soje suggested desperately.

"Yes, that's a good idea, the night air will definitely do her good", Gbaja agreed excitedly, "let's get moving."

You are both insane if you think I'm going anywhere at 2.am!" Alero retorted. How can you even suggest that!

"I'm beginning to think you guys are the ones with the fever."

She had been nothing but polite and impeccably mannered since they found her two weeks earlier and the man did not take any offence at her harsh tone; if anything, it only added to their concern for her welfare. This was not the Alero they had become so used to. She had become a beloved little sister, and object of their collective dreams, and they would have done anything to save her.

She tried to laugh.

It was just a few minutes past 10pm but no one cared to correct Alero. It did not matter anyhow. It may well have been 2am. They had been holed up for what seemed like forever, and the danger and hunger was threatening their collective sanity.

"I will go outside to gather some herbs."

Everyone turned in the direction of the usually taciturn Timmy. They could barely make out each other's features in the almost complete darkness, but it was clear from his tone that his mind was made up.

"Timmy that would be a crazy action to take right now."

Alero tried to protest through teeth that shook so badly it sounded as if she they would tumble out of her mouth any minute.

"Oga Jide, please let me go. I promise I will be

careful. I was the person that plucked the last set of herbs and I know just where to go." No one bothered to correct him that Jide had picked the last set.

Jide was torn. Timmy made a lot of sense. But as the leader of the rapidly dwindling group, he was reluctant to give any approval that could lead to the loss of another man. They had already lost three men within a few days, and he was trying very hard to shove down the guilt he felt over their deaths.

The men had been killed within hours of each other while trying to get help for some of the few remaining villagers in Yemowei. They had paid the ultimate price for humanity and hopefully for the greater good of their country. Recently Jide had found himself almost questioning his beliefs in the future of his country.

Stuck in a hole in the ground far from home and any semblance of comfort, he had allowed his mind to wander to the futility of the cause for which they believed and gave their precious lives. But was it really futile? Young men like Timmy who constantly stepped up to the plate to do what needed to be done often gave him hope that all would be well one day. Right now, he was torn between watching the young girl die and allowing one of his best men risk his life to save her. It was a hard choice. There was no guarantee the herbs would provide the much-needed relief, on the other hand, the danger outside their hole-in-the-ground was not in doubt. If Timmy died in the quest for the herbs, he would not only die, but likely, they would all be rounded up and killed as well, including Alero. On the other hand, if Alero died from whatever was ailing her, they would all blame themselves for not trying hard enough.

"Tim, we appreciate your concern; we are all concerned for Alero but we both know what's likely out there. How do you intend to make your way in the dark?"

"Sir, let me go. I won't need light. Once my eyes adjust to the darkness outside, I can make my way to the spot where I picked the last set."

"And if you get caught?"

"Tell my mother I love her."

And with that he was gone. He crawled very quickly and silently from the hole in the ground that had been their home for the past few days. It was one of the numerous burrowed pits that various petroleum exploration companies had dug in the area several years earlier.

The large pits were never filled in when they were no longer useful, and they dotted the landscape in the entire region. In the rainy season they were a haven for mosquitoes as they filled with rainwater which was useless for anything because of the pollution from the crude oil residue. Thankfully, this was the dry season. The only danger was from animals that sometimes fell into the pits. This one had been naturally covered at one end by foliage and debris from the forest around and had provided perfect cover for Jide and his band of fugitives. They had even managed to make it a little bit more hospitable by digging it in a little further when they had sensed the danger lurking outside.

It had begun to feel like their home in the jungle, and now it was in danger. How long would it be before Timmy was caught and they were exposed? It seemed like a long night lay ahead.

2

He stared in fascinated horror at the stump twitching on the ground. He looked at the faces of the men around him wondering why they all looked so strange.

Then he looked down at the red puddle gathering at his feet and spreading rapidly in a snaking line towards one of his assailants. He opened his mouth to scream, and a loud gurgling sound came out pushing a hot torrent of vomit straight into the face of the man who had just chopped off his left hand. He felt something close to satisfaction as the black earth rushed to meet him. Moments before he hit the ground, his last conscious thought was of his beloved piano. Would he ever play again?

Tofumando sputtered in rage as he wiped the

vomit off his face; the boys knew better than to stand close to him. He could turn on any one of them at any moment. They pretended to hurry around looking for water for him to wash his face.

They were all secretly pleased at what they regarded as just punishment. The young soldier had presented no direct threat to them. They didn't have to maim him for life. It would have been enough to beat him and let him be; he was obviously lost and there was no reason to doubt his story. But Tofumando did not care for such stories. He believed no one and lived for no one. He was totally brutal and though he demanded complete loyalty from his boys, he gave it to none.

They had broken away from the main faction of the Niger-Delta Liberation group about a year ago when he perceived that their leader was "weakening" and leaning towards a peaceful resolution of the crisis. Tofumando had no stomach for peace. He loved to fight, the bloodier the better. To him, a fight meant power, money and women (not necessarily in that order). He was willing to do anything illegitimate to get any or all three. The only god he believed in was his belly.

He served no one's interests but his own. He had never been married but he had women spread across the creeks who were either willing to do his bidding or were forced to do so. To him sex was a way of relieving himself and he did it as easily as he did everything else in life. He had no feelings for the women he took and used and abused.

He raped as easily as he ate, and he had sired countless number of urchins in the creeks. These meant nothing to him. No one had claims of any sort on him. He was a rebel to the core.

It was rumoured that his father who had been a catechist in the Anglican Church had cursed him on his death bed several years earlier when Tofumando was a mere teenager. It was a story no one dared ask him about. The other story that nobody wanted to confirm was the reason he had become evil in the first place. The story was that his mother had fallen ill while they were alone on a fishing trip when he was a little boy. There had been nobody to help boy carry his sick mother and he had dragged her across the creeks till he got to where their little boat was anchored. By the time he paddled the canoe to their village to ask for help the woman had died. He had flipped, blaming himself and everybody for her death. He had dropped out of school and run away from home for many years. By the time he came back, he had become a notorious political thug and real-life monster.

He had started his inglorious career as a political thug for politicians who were running for office. Then he graduated to armed robbery, kidnapping, arson and blowing up oil pipelines. His police file was several inches thick, but no one could keep him in jail. The Police knew that he was more trouble than he was worth, and they silently prayed for an opportunity to silence him or that one of his boys would turn on him and do the job. No such opportunity had come yet though there had been several attempts in the past. Those who attempted never got the chance to try it again.

He was one of those criminals everyone knew but no one did anything to tame. The security agents who had tried to rein him in in years past did not live to tell the story. So, he was left alone to rule the creeks at will. Tofumando was not the sort of man you threatened. His name was a dreaded whisper in the creeks; it was used to calm crying babies and hissed at stubborn boys everywhere.

"May you not grow up to be like Tofumani the useless one" an exasperated mother would often say to a stubborn child. But no one could be like him. He was completely evil, and his boys had witnessed it enough times to live in dread of him. None showed their fear though. He thrived on the fear of others and if he sensed that any of his boys was afraid of him, they would be slaughtered without mercy and cannibalised on the spot.

They all had to act brave, which explained why no one had attempted to stop him when it became clear he was about to maim the soldier. Oproza finally pulled off his shirt and handed it to him to finish wiping off the vomit.

"Master, make I finish am abi make I leave am to finish im blood for ground here?" the juju wey dey dis place go happy to swallow dis fresh blood small small o!"

The suggestion that the young soldier be allowed to bleed to death was a dicey one; it could be interpreted as cowardice. In fact, coming from anyone else, it would be interpreted as treachery, but not Oproza. He matched his master in meanness and the others were a little surprised at the suggestion. Oproza believed in swift killing and had in fact suggested they kill the soldier outright when he was first captured. His allusion to the gods of the place was the only plausible explanation. He was as fetish as his master, and they often engaged in all sorts of rituals ostensibly to appease the gods and increase their own power. Tofumando grunted in disgust and stood over the unconscious soldier; he unzipped his trousers and proceeded to empty his bladder on the young man's head.

"Oya, make all of una come piss for im body. If na shit sef, naim better pass! Yeye boy. I tink say e get power. Juju go gree take dis one blood sef?" He spat on him for good measure as the boys hurriedly unzipped their trousers and urinated all over the soldier. Oproza positioned himself over the boy's stump and urinated directly on the wound which was already attracting insects.

Tofumando was already moving away but the younger boys exchanged furtive glances. They often used their urine as disinfectant for open wounds and they wondered why Oproza was disinfecting the soldier's wound. Did he have a plan for the boy to survive? He had behaved out of character twice within a short period and they wondered what he was up to, but no one dared to question him. The law of the jungle is not kind to those who speak out of turn, hierarchy was respected. You didn't voice your thoughts unless you were invited to do so. In any case, Tofumando was already striding away from the young soldier with Oproza hard at his heels. The boy would be history in a few minutes. Without looking back, he barked out fresh instructions, "Make una no kill am. Carry am for ground make we dey go. E go tell us where im comot for inside this bush."

Timmy could feel the life draining from him. His life flashed before him like a movie; his days as a barefooted young boy, running around almost naked in his neighbourhood in Sapele. He was the bastard son of a single mother who sold oranges and bananas in the local market for a living. In his home, food was scarce, luxury was non-existent, and discipline was intermittent. His mother was constantly torn between giving him a good beating and allowing him to have his way so he would not run away from home. he had tried it before when he was only eight years old. She had beaten him for getting into a fight and injuring one of the neighbourhood kids. His response was to run away from home. it had taken five days of diligent search by the Police before they found him wandering the streets in Oghareki, a small town several kilometres away. He was hungry, tired and clearly frightened. He had spent the days wandering the streets and begging for crumbs from strangers and at night he had slept under tables in the marketplace by the jetty.

When the Police examined him, he said he had run away from his mother's beating and gone to the wharf where they often played. He knew his mother would likely search for him there, so he had slipped into one of the boats anchored to the jetty. These boats were built up wooden structures that housed whole families and which moved around the region trading in seafood. They would move from one riverside town to the other, and their goods usually consisted of crabs, shrimps, crayfish, and scaly fish which was caught fresh and smoked right on the boat. Whole families lived on these boats, and sometimes be in the port for several weeks at a time until their goods were all sold. Unfortunately for Timmy, the boat he ran into that day had finished its business and was leaving that night. He hid under a pile of clothes and promptly fell asleep. He woke up the following day with a rumbling stomach and no idea where he was.

Timmy had been a model child after that incident. He had missed his mother too much and he did not want to experience that level of fear again, but his mother had to return to the markets to sell her oranges. And the streets were beckoning, the streets were always beckoning and an eight-year-old left on his own was powerless to resist the allure. Timmy succumbed. After a few weeks he was back on the streets, fighting, stealing, running. He was a pupil in the neighbourhood primary school and his grades were always above average, but Timmy was restless, and he found school quite boring. He was good with numbers, and he soon fell in with a gang of cardplayers. They played a variant of poker known locally as "jogba" he was so adept at dealing cards he was soon winning bets from older boys. He would win, and they would beat him and collect the money back from him, then a fight would ensue. But the next day he would be back, bruised and sometimes battered but he got better and better and beat the more established young gamblers until they gradually gave him his respect. He was nicknamed, "Timmy jogba."

By the time Timmy hit ten years, he was not only an established gambler, he had his own little gambling business set up. He had boys who played jogba in other neighbourhoods and brought him returns. The law of the streets was respected, he was a king in his own right. No one dared cross him. His mother was not happy, but she could say or do nothing, Timmy had become a man before his time, he was making more money from gambling than she was making selling oranges and whenever she confronted him, he was quick to remind her of the fact.

"Mama, abeg, if my wahala too much for you, just tell me make I find my way. This no be like las time wey I run and Police come find me. If I comot this time I no go ever come back. I get my own dough now. I no kill person, no be only me stubborn for this Oguanja, I no tiff, na only jogba I dey play."

She had nothing to say in response. Timmy continued his thriving jogba business.

* * * * *

Hot searing pain shot through Timmy's hand to every cell in his body. The childhood movie of his life faded rapidly into one big mass of pain, and he broke out in sweat at the effort to refrain from crying out in pain. The men had carried him for a while but were now pulling him along a relatively smooth bush path. The discomfort from being pulled along like a sack of potatoes was what woke him up. His only hope of surviving lay in his ability to keep calm and gather as much information about his captors and his surroundings as possible so he kept his mouth tightly closed and tried to maintain a steady breathing. He had no idea how long he been out when he lost consciousness, but he prayed it had not been too long. The further away they moved from the point where he was captured the more difficult it would be to find his way back.

They soon came to a small clearing in the woods

and the men dropped him and moved closer to the centre of the clearing. Timmy strained to catch a word of the discussion going on a few feet away, but it was futile. The gang leader seemed to be addressing his men. He was speaking a mixture of broken English and the local Ijaw dialect. Timmy and the rest of the men had taken a crash course in Ijaw before the start of the mission, but between the stress of the past few weeks and the agony he was currently feeling, he could not make out the words. He felt hot and cold at the same time and was afraid he would pass out again. He tried to be quiet, but he must have let out a whimper because Tofumandu seemed to realize they had an intruder in their midst.

"Dis yeye boy never die?

"Oya, Oproza, kill am make we roast im body chop for here"

Cannibalism was only one the many unusual practices he took delight, and though most of his followers balked at the thought of eating a fellow human beig, they knew better than to argue with the boss.

"Oga Tofu, na dis one wey be like wetin dem take serve juju you wan make we chop?"

"Let me jus kill am trowey for dis bush, time no

dey to even roast anytin now oh!"

Again, Oproza was the only one who dared to oppose Tofumandu. The others were even more puzzled but as usual nobody said anything.

"Oya, Opro, finish am make we dey go."

With that he turned away and the men followed rapidly. Oproza stayed behind to finish off the young soldier. He was deputy king of the jungle; he would catch up with them in no time.

He waited till his comrades were out of earshot, then he bent down and began to talk to Timmy.

3

The tension in their little hideout was so thick you could almost touch it. Although they could not hear everything that was going on outside, they had heard enough to know that their brave friend and colleague was in major trouble. In fact, from that last guttural scream they'd heard, they were all sure he was no longer on this side of heaven, and they mourned as one. Aside the special bond they had all formed as a result of being forced to live in a hole like animals he was truly a special guy. His quiet and dignified manner had been a calming influence on everyone since the start of the mission. He never complained, always did his share, and frequently volunteered for the most unpleasant tasks. He ate very little, spoke even less and spent a lot of time praying quietly. They would miss him terribly.

Jide took it the hardest. He blamed himself for allowing the young man to go out and risk his life. As the leader of the small and slowly diminishing group he should have been the one to go out. At the time it had seemed like a bright idea to allow Tim to be the one to go because he was slight of frame and light footed and could be trusted to move silently. Now Jide could not help but wonder if he had not been taking the easy way out by allowing them to persuade him to remain in the bunker while the younger man took his place. Had he really been too scared to face whatever was out there? He felt a deep sense of shame and all he could see through the eyes of his grief was a man who was not fit to be called a leader. Thankfully for the group, Jide was wise enough to hold his thoughts firmly locked in his head. The rest of them were too grief-stricken to notice the war that was raging within him anyway, so he held his peace and dealt with his demons the best way he knew, by being useful. He got up and checked Alero's temperature and was alarmed to see that she was burning up again severely, worse than before, and she had started to shiver again.

This was hardly surprising considering the trauma of the last few minutes. He did not need anyone to tell him that if this little lady died, they were all gone. Taking care of her had become the most important job in the world for all four men in the past two weeks since they had been driven underground by the insurgents.

She was their queen, their star and mascot rolled into one. And she had been brave, too! In fact, she had shown a lot of courage and had complained very little, sharing whatever little food they found and helping to make their little hole-in-the-ground home more comfortable. She had become wife, mother, big sister and little sister. Jide knew that half the men secretly crushed on her. As for him, he had realized in the past two weeks that if he could not marry this girl then there was no wife in his future. He had not said anything of course; his job was to get them off this island and then everything else would follow. At least that had been the plan until four days ago when the fever hit her, and it seemed like she might not follow them out of this hell hole. The concern for her wellbeing was the major reason the young man had insisted so strongly that he be allowed to leave the hideout and venture out. And now it seemed like their little band had been reduced even further. And from the way she was shivering, Alero could be gone before morning. The gloom descended even deeper over him.

He tried to listen carefully for any sign of life from outside and he heard nothing. But he knew better than to venture out, the militants could very well be waiting for someone like him to attempt a rescue so they could swoop on the rest of them. He had been involved in guerrilla warfare long enough to know the drill. His personal sense of failure notwithstanding, he knew that their only hope for survival depended on his ability to keep his wits and make the right judgment so he waited and prayed that she would make it through the night.

He undressed her to her undergarments and tried to settle her more comfortably. The fact that she allowed him to undress her was another indication of how weak she had become. The rest of them were too scared and grief stricken to focus their minds on anything amoral. They just wanted her to get better so they would not have to mourn her as well as Tim their gentle friend who surely had been killed a few meters away from their hideout. It was a deeply sober group that sat and waited for the approaching death in that tropical hell.

4

Jide woke up with a start. What was that sound? He looked around in the darkness at the three men asleep in various positions. For a moment he was disoriented and wondered why there were three instead of four men around him. Then the events of the past few hours came rushing back at him with full force and all vestiges of sleep immediately fled from his eyes.

Tim was gone! And Alero, their beloved little lady, was she still alive? Was she the one who had made the noise that woke him up? He could not even recall falling asleep. The stress of the past hours must have overwhelmed him at some point. He had no idea what time it was and he dared not reach for his wristwatch in the dark until he was sure what had woken him up. He stretched out his hand in the dark and felt for her face. As he did, she reached out and gripped his hand very tightly. He was relieved to feel the fever appeared to have abated slightly and her grip in the dark was firm. She seemed to be trying to communicate something to him and he went still. She felt for his face and pressed her fingers to his lips for silence.

At that moment he heard it again. A dry rustling sound that came and went. Yes, the sound came from above and from all indications it was a living thing. The first and immediate thought was that their hideout had been found and the militants were coming for them. That was the only explanation that made sense. Or was it? Why would they want to come for them in the dead of night? But then again what could it be? A wild beast?

They had encountered none in the past few weeks since they had been stranded in the jungle. It was as if the wild animals had run away at the start of this war that seemed to have no end. So, what could it be? These random thoughts raced through Jide's mind as he listened hard for the sound. Alero quietly sat up and moved closer to where he was. He made as much room for her as he could and held her hand tightly to reassure her as much as himself. There was the sound again and this time there was no doubt it was headed in their direction. Whoever was making the sound was being careful and was obviously trying to be quiet. This time Jide was no longer in doubt, it had to be the militants. They had somehow managed to locate their hideout and were attempting to kill them in their sleep.

A deep sense of calm came over him and he thought briefly about their options. They had run out of ammunition long ago and the knives they had were no match for the sophisticated weapons he knew the militants carried. All his men were accomplished martial artists but he knew they were too weakened by hunger and lack of exercise to be of any use to themselves. All the same he decided he would wake them up to face the enemy rather than allow them to be slaughtered in their sleep. He knew his men would rather die fighting and in fact would welcome the chance to take a last stand. He tried to wake them quietly without making any noise. Alero quickly caught on to what he was trying to do and soon all three of them were sitting up and alert. They deliberately slowed their breathing down using martial arts techniques, and soon the hideout was silent as a graveyard while they waited for the sound of the enemy from above. When it came, it was much closer than they expected, they braced themselves for the assault. They had taken what positions they could with the lady behind them and this time Jide was in front, he wanted to take the first bullet if it came to it. He was not going to allow any more of his men to be killed while he stood aside. They waited again for what seemed like hours, but which could not really have been much more than a few minutes. When the next sound came, they were too shocked to immediately react. It was a long slow bird whistle, a sound which all four of them had heard from Tim several times in the past few weeks.

A sound he claimed he had learnt as a child and had never forgotten. A sound they had jokingly referred to as Tim's call of nature. Was it possible? Could he be the one? Was he alive? Or was it a trick? Jide was sure it was Tim out there, but he also concluded that it had to be a trick. The militants must have forced him to their hideout and were now trying to use him to lure them out.

He shook his head silently in the dark. So, this was the end? He felt a passing sadness for his mother. But he did not really dwell on it. He had learnt long ago from a wise man that a man's dying thoughts should always focus on the hereafter and not on the world he was leaving behind. So, he turned his thoughts to eternity as he waited for whatever was coming at him. Would he go to this heaven they spoke about? Somehow, he did not think so. He knew without any doubt that he had lived his life for himself and would go to hell if there was such a thing. His mother had repeatedly tried to get him to make a commitment to live for Jesus Christ, but Jide had always insisted that he was alright and did not need religion.

"Christianity is not religion my son," she had told him often, but he had just laughed. Of course, it was religion! What else could it be? He admired what his Mum had and knew it was real, he just did not feel ready for it. And now far from home in the creeks, away from all he knew and loved, the question of eternity was glaring him in the face and he wondered if he could make it right with God in the few moments he had left. The whistle came again but this time it did not stop. It was urgent and insistent, and it was coming closer. He seemed to be warning them of his approach and they all instinctively shrank back deeper into their hole, pressing into one another. Suddenly, their makeshift door of leaves and twigs swung open, and Tim slid to the floor in front of them!

They were in shock for all of five seconds before

they could react. And then they all pounced on him in mixed emotions. "Shh, shh," he motioned for silence and tried to scramble away from them in the dark.

"I am badly injured," he informed them through clenched teeth, "but we have to go away immediately. They will come back to this area soon and we must move tonight."

He quickly brought them up to speed about what had taken place while he was away. He had wandered a little farther away than he had planned in search of herbs and water for Alero's fever and was returning from the bush when he had heard the voices of the militants heading straight for him. There had been no time to run or hide so he quickly tossed the plastic bottle of water into the bush. Unfortunately, the sound of the bottle hitting the ground had also alerted the group heading towards him that there was someone in front of them and he had narrowly missed being shot to pieces. Subsequently, they had dragged him deeper into the bush and tortured him for close to an hour before his hand was chopped off mercilessly. He had been left to bleed to death. But for some reason which can only be the hand of God, they had carried him along with them unconscious deeper into the jungle. At some point there had been a brief debate about whether he should be roasted for dinner or sacrificed to the gods of the jungle.

Finally, one of them had been designated to finish him off and make sure he was dead. Rather than finish him off, he had bandaged his stump with herbs and a dirty rag to stop the bleeding and given him a concoction from a little bottle he attached to his trousers to drink. The evil-smelling brew was obviously alcoholic, and Tim had almost choked but he had been forced to swallow a huge gulp. His throat burnt and his head felt like it would explode but after a few minutes, the throbbing in his hand seemed to ease a little and he could focus a bit better. He had never tasted alcohol in his twenty-plus years, not even when he lived as a stubborn little boy with his mother in Sapele. He was sure he was drunk because the man was whispering instructions to him on how he could escape. He told him he had to find his way quickly out of the bush where they were because they were coming back to make camp in that area, and he would surely be killed if they found him on their return. He ended his instructions by saying, "you just be like my small broda, and I no go fit just let you die like that,"

They were all stunned at what they heard, and it was then they noticed that his hand was in a dirty makeshift bandage, and he truly seemed to be in a lot of pain. There were swollen welts all over his body and his head was broken and bloody in several places. But there was no time to dwell on pity if what he had just related was anything to go by.

They hurriedly gathered up their very meagre belongings and prepared to move out. Jide looked around to ensure they had left nothing behind that would give clues to whoever stumbled on their hole. It was difficult to erase the evidence left behind by footprints and body impressions, but he made sure nothing else remained. As they made to move out, Tim held them back and insisted they pray and commit their hazardous trip into God's hands. Jide was more than a little impatient but then he recalled how he had felt a short while ago when he was sure that his life had come to an end! He mentally shook his head. They crawled out of the hole one person at a time, trying to be quiet and quick at the same time. It was almost pitch-black outside, the stars seemed to have gone into hiding from this senseless war in the creeks. Once out of the hole, Jide offered to lead but Tim brushed him aside.

"I have a better idea of where we are supposed to go and we should be as quiet as possible, so I cannot be directing you. I think I should lead and have

Alero and Soje follow me closely behind while you and Gbaja bring up the rear."

The arrangement could not be faulted, and they set off at a brisk pace, stopping occasionally to get their bearing. They were heading in the opposite direction from where they had come, and the going was slow and laborious in the dark. It was also clear that Tim was in a lot of pain, and he had to be careful so he would not hit his stump against a tree in the dark.

Jide suggested they stop so Tim could rest a bit, but he would hear none of it. They must have stumbled in the dark for what seemed like hours before Jide insisted that they stop because he realized Alero was slowing down very frequently. Tim finally gave in and collapsed to the ground as soon as they stopped. Jide felt his forehead for his temperature and was alarmed to see that he seemed to be burning up. Thankfully though, the fresh air seemed to have stabilised Alero as her body was cooler to the touch. But she was obviously exhausted from the gruelling march in the dark. He also examined Tim's stump which had been giving him cause for major concern. He had been wondering if the wound was bleeding and leaving trails for any would-be pursuers to follow in the light of day. He was relieved to see that the bandage was holding, and the hand was not bleeding. Tim seemed to read his thoughts.

"He told me the hand would not bleed for about twelve hours, and that is why we must hurry. If we don't get help soon, the bleeding will resume, and I will surely die." The matter-of-fact way he said it sent chills down the spines of his hearers and they stood up as one, ready to move on again.

"But how can we be sure we are moving in the right direction in this darkness?"

"I know we are because I've been praying. I know the Spirit of God has been guiding us." No one felt like arguing with him as they wearily dragged themselves up and continued walking in the dark. After a while, Tim stopped abruptly, and they all bumped into one another. He held up his hand for silence.

Soon they all heard what he must have heard, a gurgling sound like running water somewhere ahead. No doubt there was a stream or a brook of some sort ahead. They continued cautiously with Tim stopping frequently. The sound was much nearer now, and the ground felt softer. The air was also noticeably cooler. Finally, Tim stopped and motioned for them sit down. They dropped to the ground gratefully, with Soje stretching out in full.

"He advised we wait here till we can see our way to

cross the stream as it is quite high in some places and there is no sense drowning in the dark. He also said there are snakes around the stream, so we need to be very careful where we sit or lie." At that Soje sprang up from where he lay and moved closer to Jide.

Jide finally brought out his illuminated watch from his pocket and it was well past 4am! He had not checked the time they set out, but he was sure they had been on the move for at least four hours. Tim answered his unspoken thoughts; "he had told me it would take me about four hours to get to the stream but of course he did not know I would not be alone, and he did not factor in the time I spent in getting you guys so I reckon we have been moving for about five or six hours now. Also judging from the pain, I feel, whatever was in that concoction must be wearing off, so yes, I guess, it must be about six hours since I left him."

They were hungry and thirsty but that was the least of their problems right now. They were faced with a new challenge as they tried to find somewhere to sit more comfortably. Mosquitoes! They came in droves and settled on every bit of exposed skin. Everyone was soon slapping away except for Tim who not only had no hand to slap but was in so much pain that he could not add to it by slapping himself.

He just moved his head from side to side and tried to put his good hand over his face as much as possible. Alero was making little moaning sounds and Soje had sat up and was sticking his head between his knees in a bizarre attempt to shield his face. Jide was sure their misery could not get any worse!

5

Finally, the sky seemed to lighten, and daybreak reluctantly crept on the little band of miserable refugees. The birds were beginning to sing in the trees above and they began to stretch aching and bruised limbs. The past two hours had to be amongst the most miserable yet of their nightmarish existence in the past few weeks. As the light increased, they could see that Alero looked pale and almost ready to drop with fatigue and the remnants of whatever was ailing her. Tim was obviously in a lot of pain and trying unsuccessfully to hide it and the rest of them looked equally miserable. As they looked around their mosquito infested surroundings, Jide made a silent pledge that if they got out of the creeks alive, he would worship this God of his mother and Tim forever. The situation looked as bleak as could be and he just did not think they had the strength to make it out of there alive. Although Tim looked worse than all of them, he appeared to be the most optimistic. He again insisted they pray before setting out on their quest.

"We need to move carefully till we get to the part of the stream that is shallow enough to wade across and then we go across and get further into the creeks."

"And then what?" Soje wanted to know.

"How do we know the shallow end? And when we cross, assuming we do not drown or get swallowed up by a croc, what happens next? Who is waiting for us on the other side, ehn?"

His panic was making his voice shrill and it was clear the tension, fatigue and the endless hunger was beginning to take its toll.

"Don't worry my brother, maybe it is pointless, maybe it is not, but whatever happens, at least we are doing something about our getting away from this island."

Soje began to weep, gently at first, and before long he was heaving great sobs of pain and anguish that reached down to everyone's soul.

Jide allowed it for a few moments but soon realised that if he did not put a stop to it, the crying would demoralise them even further.

"Put a stop to that stupidity right now, or I will drown you myself!" he pretended to be angrier than he felt. "You are a soldier, and you knew the risks involved when you signed up. Don't disgrace your commission by acting like a bloody coward. We are men; we fight for what we believe in. That is what we are trained for. This is enemy territory and we owe it a duty to ourselves and our nation to do everything to make it out alive. We are together in this, and we have come too far to let ourselves down. If we have to die in the process, then so be it, but we remain dignified to the very end. There will be no more crying, complaining, or grumbling of any sort. Is that understood?"

His voice was much harsher than they had ever heard it, but it had the desired effect. They sobered up immediately. Even Alero seemed to stand a little straighter. They continued along the bank in silence, keeping within the bushes so they could not be spotted by a careless observer. Soon Tim called a halt and walked to the edge of the stream. He stooped down, scooped a handful of water with one hand and splashed it over his face.

"I think we can cross from here. And maybe we should try to freshen up a bit too."

He continued splashing water on his face and on his head. He tried to wash off as much blood as he could from the less swollen part of his face. Soon the others joined him and the refreshing coolness of the water on their skin seemed to heighten their thirst.

"Do you think it is safe to drink?" Soje asked fearfully.

His voice was hoarse with thirst and weeping and he looked longingly at the water.

"I would not advise it. The villagers drink it obviously, but we know it cannot be too safe, maybe further up where it is a bit clearer"

Jide did not like the way Soje was looking. The fight seemed to have gone out of him, which was rather surprising considering that he had been so brave and stoic all along. You never really know what a man is capable of until he is tested under intense pressure! Jide kept his concerns to himself as he surveyed the bank with Tim. Tim had proved to be the hero of the group without a doubt. From the way he held his stump it was clear that he was in a lot of pain. Jide recalled the snatches of conversation he had with the young man during training, about his rough past; it was clear he was much tougher than he looked. Growing up in the ghetto must have had its benefits after all. He was clearly in agony. His face was puckered up in seeming concentration, but Jide guessed it was more pain than anything else. Yet he showed no other signs of it. He was focusing on his self-assigned role of assistant leader and scout. Jide picked some loose pieces of wood and felt for the bottom of the stream.

"I believe we can cross here; it is quite firm, and it appears relatively shallow all the way across." This time he took the lead. Tim was behind, and Alero was between the other two people with Soje bringing up the rear, they waded across slowly in single file. Jide heaved a big sigh of relief as the last man climbed out of the water on the other side. Although it had taken them no more than fifteen minutes to wade across the stream, it was harrowing all the same. If anyone had come upon them they would have been sitting ducks!

"I think we should move away from the direction where we crossed and go further into the creeks" He suggested.

"I agree with you. The man that helped me said we should move up towards the rising sun and we would come to a friendly village before noon, but we have to be careful in entering the village to be sure that they have not been compromised or invaded. It's his village but he says he has not been home for over six months now."

As they talked, they moved in an easterly direction, making as good a speed as could be made in the creeks. The trees grew close together and their twisted winding trunks often had long thick ropes spreading from tree to tree, making movement slower than they would have liked.

It was much closer to the stream, and more dangerous. Jide's main concern was for Tim and Alero. Although the water appeared to have revived Alero a bit, but she still looked very frail. He knew the rigours of trekking through the night in hunger and thirst, coupled with the assault from the mosquitoes had taken their toll on her already weakened frame but she was trying to be brave. He was content to let sleeping dogs lie.

Tim's hand had swollen to twice its size by the time they had walked for two hours and Jide knew that if they did not get help soon, they were looking at death by gangrene infection. Tim obviously knew this too, so he was pushing harder than everyone. He was no longer talking, just clenching his jaw and pushing on relentlessly behind Jide. They had been walking for four hours when Alero suddenly slumped.

"I'm sorry, please forgive me", she whispered feebly as she tried to rise to her feet. Soje and Gbaja quickly rushed to help her up.

"We will rest a bit. There's no sense in pushing ourselves to death. We should try to regain a bit of energy for the last stretch".

"Sir, I suggest we leave Alero here with them and go ahead to explore the way ahead and see if we can locate the village." Tim was clearly in agony but still unwilling to rest.

"Great idea, except that you need to rest more than anyone else."

"I know I need to rest but if we don't get to that village soon, I will be forced to rest forever. I'm not afraid to die but imagine the effect it would have on everyone else? Besides I'm the only one who knows what to do when we eventually get to the village."

"I'm not remaining here while you two go off. We should all go together or rest together" Soje whined pitifully. He looked scared to his soaking wet boots! Before Jide could respond Gbaja took Soje by the hand and reassured the group that they would be alright. The two of them set off quickly.

They made better progress alone and soon they began to sense they must be close to the village. They were now in cultivated land, and it was obvious that human beings had passed this way recently. They moved cautiously through a cassava farm keeping their eyes open for any human sound.

6

Suddenly, Jide found himself on the ground struggling for breath! There was a vice grip on his neck, and he felt the life ebbing out of him within seconds. He heard whimpering from close by which he suspected must be coming from Tim. He could not see anything except the stars which were dancing in front of his eyes. Where and how had they come from so silently? He wondered as he flailed uselessly under his assailant. Tim was still whimpering and suddenly gasped in pain, shouting a word that made no sense to Jide. It must have been some sort of code because the grip on his neck was relaxed a bit and he opened his eyes. All he could see was the grass beneath him. His ears were on fire and ringing from pain. He felt shame down to his bones at how easily they had been captured. No wonder these people had made minced meat of the army; they were good!

His assailant sat him up, all the while standing behind him. He also could not see Tim although he could feel him a few feet away.

"Na Oproza say make we come dis side ask of Papa Tombra. Make we tell am say sake of Esaiblokemi, make dem help us comot go reach Patani."

His garbled explanation made no sense at all to Jide but then nothing made sense right now. The men discussed something between them briefly then yanked them to their feet. Jide's hands were swiftly tied behind his back in a tight knot, but Tim was allowed to hold up his now badly swollen hand. They were marched briskly along a footpath which the two men had not noticed before and suddenly they came out into a small clearing in the middle of the thick vegetation. One minute the place looked thickly forested, the next minute they were in a clearing with two adobe huts in the middle. There was no way they would have found the place on their own. They were separated, with Jide held behind one of the huts while Tim was taken inside the second hut. Jide was tied to a tree trunk and left in the sweltering heat.

Elsie O. Dennis

Soon he heard Tim crying out in agony. He could only hope and pray that it was from his stump being treated and not from further torture. After a few minutes the cries died down to a whimper and then stopped altogether. Shortly after, one of his captors brought him water in a bowl and put the bowl to his lips. He drank greedily but the bowl was lowered out of his reach just as quickly. Then it was raised to his lips again and then Jide understood. It was unwise for him to gulp all the water at once and the man wanted him to take only small sips. He sipped gratefully and mumbled "thank you." Mercifully he sank into a deep sleep.

When he woke up it was getting to dusk, and he was no longer tied outside; he was inside one of the huts. His hands were free and there was a steaming bowl of some sort of gruel in front of him. The man who had obviously woken him up pointed to the gruel and made signs that he should eat. Jide did not need a second urging, but he was worried about his people and a bit upset with himself that he had slept for so long. He must have been more tired than he realised. He looked up at the man who was partially masked and tried to enquire about his colleagues, but the man shook his head at him, motioned to him to eat and walked out. Jide was worried sick, but he also knew he needed his strength to think properly. He pulled the gruel towards himself and ate it slowly but surely. He did not know what he was eating but the taste was not bad at all. After the first few mouthfuls, he felt strength coursing through his body. In no time at all he had cleaned the plate and he would have asked for more if he knew how or where. As if he had been under observation his host slipped back into the hut, this time with another bowl of steaming hot liquid.

"Drink am small small," the man advised in tones that were neither harsh nor kind. Jide did as advised and took small sips of the obviously alcoholic but very sweet liquid. It was like nothing he had ever tasted in his life before but from the instant rush of energy he felt, he could almost swear that it was some form of narcotic mixed with alcohol and God-knows-what else. His head was swimming by the time he was done, and the man bent down, took him by the hand, and heaved him to his feet with a movement so lithe that Jide did not have time to be surprised. They were outside the hut in a blink, and it was then Jide realised it was pitch dark outside. It took him a few seconds to adjust to the darkness and to pick out the forms of his companions who were also being held by various other people.

Nobody spoke. The silence was almost deafening in the eerie darkness. He dared not ask what they were waiting for, he could hardly see beyond the little group standing in front of him. They were obviously in the middle of the mangrove forest and the only sounds were the incessant chirping of insects. He tried to recall his martial arts training and stilled his breathing to enhance his hearing. Soon he a heard a barely perceptible sound of water lapping against something. He could not be sure but then he began to suspect that they must be close to a creek or stream. As if to confirm his thoughts two men appeared from the bushes and joined the little group. They conferred with the others briefly and then gave marching orders.

"Oya make we dey go. Everibodi kwayet o! Unless una wan die for dis bush"

Jide and his little group did not need a second warning. They moved in single file into the bush path they had not known was there. He did a hurried head count in the dark and realized with relief that they were all complete. They made their way through a narrow path with large metallic barrels on either side. It was too dark to make out what it was but Jide began to suspect they were passing through one of the numerous illegal refineries rumoured to be in the area. He noticed Alero in the dark ahead of him. She seemed to be walking straighter than the last time he saw her a few hours ago and he wondered what magic herbs she had been given. What Jide did not know until much later was that they had been captured four days earlier. He thought he had only slept for a few hours when he had actually been unconscious for four whole days. In that time, they had been moved from the point of capture deeper into the mangrove forest and Alero had been treated by their captors. Tim had also received the best jungle medical care available for his hand and though he was still in pain, the immediate fear of gangrene had passed.

In a few minutes they were at the riverbank and one by one they got into a boat that look like it could not stay afloat in a bathtub, talk less of a river! Two people got in with them and before they could comprehend what was happening the little boat had pushed off and the two men were paddling upstream or downstream, Jide could not tell. Nobody uttered a word. It was not necessary. The smell of their fear did all the talking. Where were they being taken to? Were they being rescued as they hoped or was this the trip to neverland? Were there crocodiles in the water? What if the little boat capsized? A myriad of questions without answers. After a few minutes, by an unspoken agreement they settled down to enjoy as much of the dark and silent boat ride as possible. At least the air was fresh, and the breeze was gentle and soothing. None of them fell asleep or even dozed off. They were all alert, probably too tense to feel sleepy. Their oarsmen remained taciturn, and it was clear that conversation would not be welcome, so they were all left to their individual thoughts. Jide tried to look around in the dark but there was really nothing to see. It was pitch black and he could not fathom how they could be paddling with such dexterity. How could they be sure they were heading in the right direction? He tried not to think too much about what the implications were if they were lost. Besides, there was nothing he could do about it. He did not have the foggiest idea of where they supposed to be going to.

He cast his mind back to the very different journey he had made to this region several weeks earlier. He had been loaded with all kinds of fancy equipment and 'toys.' He had GPS, all manners of knives and a hundred different Knick knacks that he felt sure would put him five steps ahead of every militant in the creeks. He remembered how he had boasted that he could tell from a mile away what any militant had taken for breakfast. He had been so cocky! He was so sure of himself and his supposed knowledge of the Niger Delta. He had read all there was to read and had spent countless hours poring over maps. They had spent several weeks training in all manner of jungle survival techniques until he had felt he knew all there was to know. How wrong he had been! He recalled his instructor telling him that no matter how ready he felt he was, he could never be ready enough to survive the surprises the jungle could throw at you. And how Jide had scoffed! Now he felt nothing but a deep sense of shame and regret.

He had excelled in everything during the training and had almost become arrogant. He wished now that he had a way of apologizing to his instructor; a man who had learnt survival, not in the classroom and simulated jungle trainings, but in the death fields of Vietnam or Saigon as it was known then. The man had survived the Vietnamese war and had escaped capture in such unlikely circumstances that he instantly became a legend when he eventually made it back to the United States of America. He had then dedicated his life to training individuals and groups on how to survive in the jungle. He was a quiet man who hardly spoke unless there was no other option. His strength lay in his ability to communicate without saying a word. He was so strong he could lift a man twice his weight and height off the ground without breaking a stride. Jide had developed a deep respect for the man during their six weeks training and he wished he could see him once more. He was sure the man would have figured out a way to get out of the creeks several weeks ago! Jide could not help but marvel at how the whole saga had become the nightmare it was. They had started this mission so sure of victory. Jide had never failed at anything in life. He had been at the top of his class from the time he started kindergarten. And he had always wanted to be in the military, like his father before him. His mother had begged him and even his father had told him several times to choose his own path in life, but he was adamant. His path in life was the military. His parents had left him alone when they saw he could not be dissuaded and so far, everything he had done showed he truly was following his dream and no one else's. Jide was born a soldier.

7

They had been flown in a military helicopter from Lagos to Warri in the Niger Delta region in the dead of night after receiving final instructions. The small band of elite fighters had been laden with all kinds of sophisticated military equipment and the cocky enthusiasm often associated with the inexperienced but well-educated individual. You could not describe Jide as inexperienced, but his previous victories seemed to have made him a little too sure of himself. An unmarked Military van had been waiting to take them into the jungle and they had travelled over rough jungle terrain for the better part of the night. Shortly before dawn they arrived at a camp site deep in the jungle. They were deep in the heart of the mangrove forest and the silence had been deafening when the driver turned off the engine of the Military van. It was pitch black though it was close to dawn. No one moved or said anything for a full five minute after the engines were turned off. They seemed to be waiting for a signal of some sort. After a few minutes that seemed like an eternity, the driver opened his door and alighted from the van. He had not uttered one word for the entire three-hour duration of the drive into the jungle.

"Oya make all of una come down from the motor."

He had spoken in little more than a whisper, but it sounded like a bellow in the eerie pre-dawn silence. The fighters slipped down silently from the vehicle and gratefully stretched limbs that were beginning to cramp just a little bit, more from the tension than from any real discomfort. They clustered around the driver as he continued to whisper instructions in Pidgin English. Pidgin was the lingua franca in these parts and the fighters had been warned before they departed Lagos. In fact, a considerable part of their training had been done in Pidgin just to be sure they understood the importance of what it represented to the people. They had also been taught in Ijaw language, though just enough to not be completely lost.

A few more whispered instructions and the driver

got into the van and backed away into the rapidly disappearing night. They spent only a few seconds looking after the vehicle before they melted into the jungle and began the first of many long treks in very hostile territory.

From the rigorous training they had just completed the men knew the jungle they were in, and they had very sophisticated navigational equipment. They knew exactly how long it should take from the drop off point to the edge of the village that was their first point of call. But no amount of training could adequately prepare one for the realities of the dangerous jungle.

During training you knew it was all simulated and no matter what happened you could always call a halt if it got too tough, although few people ever did. But here in the actual jungle, the sense of danger was real and was heightened by every snap of a twig or chirp of a bird. The men had nerves of steel, but the experience was still nerve-racking. They moved steadily for another three hours before deciding to camp not too far from the village. It was well past 9am but the visibility in the mangrove swamp was close to zero. The village had been all but deserted when they eventually went in. All the men long gone and a lot of the women too. The militants had raided the community and made away with the best of everything. They had left the old and infirm and they had left them to starve. There was no food to be had anywhere. The hardest sight for the men had been the malnourished children with their bloated bellies and sore-festered bodies.

The small band of fighters quickly set about restoring some sort of order to the village. They had come equipped with protein tablets and some essential drugs which they quickly shared among the most vulnerable, which was almost everybody. Within the first three days they had buried five people who had died quietly, apparently from a combination of malnourishment and despair.

Jide the leader of the small group had never seen anything like this in his whole life. He realized very quickly that this mission was not going to be as cut and dried as he had hoped. They would have to change tactics if they hoped to survive to tell the tale. He split the small group into three groups of two men each and placed them at different strategic points around the village. He himself acted as coordinator, moving between the three groups and relieving whoever needed to be relieved.

Their task in Yemowei was a delicate one. Yemowei was the last strategic outpost that had not immediately fallen to the rebels in this senseless war. For some reason which was not quite clear, the rebels had seemed to have forgotten how important the little village was. Yemowei was sitting on the largest gas reserve in the entire country and until the war started it had been a peaceful little village with no signs above the ground of the prosperity that lay beneath. But it was a deliberate façade.

Yemowei was such a strategic reserve that the government had been reluctant to draw attention to it prematurely. Sons and daughters of the obscure village had quietly been offered government scholarships over the years and whisked away to school overseas and to work in the big cities.

When the fight with the rebels had continued with no sign of slowing down, this elite group had been secretly trained to provide protection for the little town and its people and to ensure that the militants kept away but apparently help had come too late.

The militants had better intelligence than they were given credit for. They knew Yemowei was important, and they knew that the government forces would eventually come.

And they waited patiently.

8

Jide was so deeply buried in his memories he did not realise the little canoe was slowing down until it had come to a complete stop. It was still pitch dark. The silence was broken by the million sounds of the night peculiar to the African jungle; the African night is never silent. Insects chirp, night-birds twit, and a hundred little creatures that are day shy often scurry around in the dark.

The combination of sounds makes the African night a very noisy one indeed. And yet it manages to be silent and forbidding at the same time. The canoe had stopped, and the men seemed to be waiting for something. Jide and his boys did not dare say anything. They could sense the tension in the night air. He wished desperately for his night vision goggles.

The place was truly pitch-black, he could not make out a form or a shadow. There was no way to tell what time of the night it was, there was neither moon nor even a star to cast some light on the inky black water. But his senses had become heightened to the presence of danger in the past few weeks since he had been in the forest and sensed rather than saw the looming danger.

He tried to still his breathing again and increase his mental alertness and that was when he heard it. A faint metallic sound that had no place in a deadly quiet creek. He could not alert his people to be prepared to die. He could only hope they had heard the sound too. The worst part was not knowing if the men with them were friends or foes. He could only hope they were the latter.

Suddenly and noiselessly the man closest to Jide touched his hand and gripped very tightly. Jide returned the pressure in what he hoped was a gesture to indicate that he understood. He was not quite sure what the man was trying to communicate though, but that gesture was enough to settle the question of whether they were in enemy hands or not, these were definitely in friendly hands.

Without appearing to move a muscle, the man lifted something close to Jide's face in the small canoe and he felt something whizz past his ear and land with a splash in the water in the direction from which they had come. Within seconds there was rapid gunfire in that direction, and it became clearer what had just taken place.

Using the sound of the gunfire as a cover the men paddled furiously further up before slowing down again to listen for more danger. The one closest to Jide dropped his paddle into the river by the side to test the depths. He leaned close to Jide and whispered in his ear that they would have to quietly slip into the water at that point.

It was more of a command than a suggestion and one by one the men slid silently into the water, it was icy cold and Alero let out an involuntary though stifled gasp. Almost immediately there was rapid gunfire in seeming response, thankfully it was still in the direction from which they had come. The men practically carried her and tried to be as silent as possible and as they swam in the direction Jide could only pray was the shore.

They were all excellent swimmers, but they did not know where they were swimming to in the inky darkness. It was all they could do to keep abreast of their benefactors. After a few minutes they started feeling the pull of the tide from the shore and then they felt the mangrove roots pulling at them from under the water.

The roots of these trees often grew deep into the riverbed and sometimes far out in the stream. In happier times they would harbour schools of fish and lucky would be the fisherman who set his net close to any of such trees, but not anymore. Between the several oil spills and the useless war that had raged in these waters for so long there was no more fish to be had anywhere.

One by one they pulled themselves out of the water and stumbled in the dark after the men who seemed to know exactly where they were going, but; how was that possible in this black dark night? Jide swore silently that if he got out of this nightmare, he would never again underestimate the intelligence of these river dwellers. Because he realised that was what had happened; the entire country had taken it for granted that because most of the people here had no formal education, they were therefore stupid. It was just beginning to dawn on everyone how wrong they had been about the creek dwellers, that they were very far from stupid.

In fact, Jide had since concluded that these creek people were not only smarter than they got credits for, but they were also in several ways smarter than the Government officials with their big titles and redundant portfolios.

These people were blessed with a natural intelligence that far outweighed whatever was taught in the best schools. They knew their region and understood the power of the elements. They knew geography, not from the pages of a textbook but from living in a rapidly changing world. A world that gave them front row seats to the consequences of climate change and global warming.

They did not need an Environmental Impact Assessment report to know that their land was no longer fit for human habitation. In a few weeks, Jide had come to question everything he had once considered important about his country. With all they had seen and felt about this land, he could not help but wonder if the larger populace had fell for a pack of carefully constructed lies.

Suddenly he bumped into the man ahead of him. He must learn to pull himself together and stop his mind from wandering so much. It appeared they had reached some level ground and he could hear the grunts and pants from behind him.

He worried about Tim and Alero. He had barely seen them since their friendly capture and though he suspected they were in much better shape he could not be sure. He wanted badly to check on them, but he also did not want to compromise their obviously precarious position by speaking.

The man in front of him touched him and gestured for him to sit down. He did the same down the line of men and one woman, touching their lips as he did so, indicating silence. They did not need much encouragement; you could almost smell the terror that hung in the air.

Jide was nothing if not brave, which was why he had been chosen to lead this mission in the first place. He had been on similar missions in the past, though nothing had been this extensive or complicated. This mission had made complete nonsense of his experience and training, now he had to rely on luck just to survive.

He had never believed in luck, often saying you created your own luck, but now he was not so sure. He found his thoughts wandering to God once again as it tended to do these days. Could it be that God was up there somewhere answering his mother's prayers? But how was it possible that the all-knowing, all-merciful God that his mother spoke about all the time would answer the prayers of people like his mother and at the same time allow this land and people to be so devastated? God did not make sense to him, in fact nothing did. If indeed there was a God somewhere, he sure had a twisted sense of right and wrong! If God was so loving and benevolent, why was there no evidence of such in these parts? What crime had they committed that had caused God to forget they even existed?

Jide felt the weariness slowly creeping over him. He tried to fight the sleep but soon he was in dreamland. He found himself dreaming of Alero. He was getting married to her in a thick forest with his mother and father present, but the priest was carrying a gun instead of a Bible and as he tried to repeat the marriage vows, he heard the voice of his commander giving him instructions on jungle warfare. Then his mother was crying and telling God to keep him safe in the bush. He felt the urge to run but he did not want to leave Alero.

Suddenly, he was in a boat alone in the middle of the sea and water was rapidly filling the boat. He tried to jump overboard and swim, but his legs were entangled in mangrove roots. Suddenly he felt a rough hand shaking him violently.

It was the last sleep that would cross his eyes for many hours.

9

He woke to the sound of rapid gunfire and whispered instructions to climb up the tree against which he leaned. There was no time to wonder what was going on; he was still scaling the tree with rapidly clearing eyes and senses when there was a staccato burst of gunfire a few feet away. This time he was sure they were all dead meat!

For the next five minutes (which seemed like an eternity) there was an unending burst of gunfire. Jide was reminded afresh of the calibre of weapons these seeming 'ragtag army' had in their possession. From the sound of the gunfire, he could tell that these were highly sophisticated, Russian-made, Pecheneg, general purpose machine guns that could fire non-stop for as long as the shooter wanted. And these shooters were determined to shoot!

The shooting stopped for a few minutes and Jide didn't know which was worse, the sound of gunfire or the eerie quiet. He expected to be shot down from his perch on the tree any moment. He was completely unarmed. Their knives had been taken away when they were rescued by Tim's strange friends and now, they were without any form of weapons at all, up on a tree in pitch blackness.

At least he was up on a tree. He had no idea what had happened to his companions and could only hope they were alright. The shooting resumed again, closer this time. Up in the tree he could not be sure if the shooters were actually coming their way or if his imagination was playing tricks on him.

He was not sure how long the shooting went on this time, but the sounds began to fade, and it became clear they were moving further away. Then the shooting stopped altogether. He wondered how long they would remain up in the tree. He did not have to wait too long.

"Oya come down make we comot for here, the yeye boy dem don go."

At first, he wondered if he was dreaming again as he heard the whispered instructions, but this was no dream. It was the captain of the boat who had asked him to climb the tree in the first place. He climbed down warily. He just could not bring himself to trust these people no matter how much they helped him and his friends. The level of brutality he had witnessed in Yemowei had convinced him that they had ice flowing in their veins.

A quick roll call in the dark assured him that they were all complete and Alero's fever seemed to have disappeared. Even Tim sounded much stronger than the last time he had seen him but there was no time to exchange pleasantries. They were quickly brought up to speed on what had just transpired.

Apparently, the rebels had come back to the area where they had left Tim to die and when they did not see his body Tofumando had immediately suspected that he had escaped. He had concluded that the young man had somehow found help and since that village was the nearest one, he had headed in that direction. Oproza knew his family would be mercilessly wiped out in an instant if he did not do something so he had sent the message ahead that they should move out. The rebels had been hot on their trail immediately they left and were still in hot pursuit.

The biggest threat to this mission was the fact that the rebels knew these creeks inside out. They had not only grown up in them but had learnt warfare in them. They knew every nook and cranny and they seemed to have their own creek communication system. Jide could find no logical explanation for how they always seemed to be several steps ahead at any point in time.

Take for instance the time they had been ambushed in Yemowei. He had been sure they had the entire village well covered; his men were well spread out in twos and the only apparent footpath into the village was being guarded but they had come upon them suddenly and killed two of his team members like chickens and then melted back into the jungle without a trace.

That had been one of the worst nights on the mission; and the worst part of it was that they could not even mourn. They had been too scared and confused, sure that the rebels would come blazing out of the bushes at any time.

Everything had been going so well. They had evacuated the village the day before when they had received reports that the militants were becoming suspicious and were likely to move in.

Yemowei was too strategic to the Government and could not be allowed to fall into the hands of the militants. The occupants of the village had also proven their loyalty to the government over the years and their rescue was of prime importance. So Jide and his elite team had arranged to have them evacuated and it had gone without a hitch.

They were sure that the mission had been a success and all they had to do was take up defensive positions and ensure that the homes of the villagers were protected while they were away. Jide had stationed his men in twos at strategic points around the village and that evening he had just finished the briefing and was on his way back to the headman's house where he had set up temporary quarters when he heard the sound that made his blood run cold.

He had changed his mind about going straight and had instead headed back to where he had started from for a final word with the boys; he was not quite sure why he had done that, but that action had probably saved him and the rest of the team. As he drew near to the little mud house, he heard the 'drip, drip' of liquid falling to the ground. He knew instinctively what it was. He froze on the spot for several seconds then slowly inched back in the direction he was coming from.

He did not know if anyone was watching, but he knew that his two colleagues that he left only a few minutes ago were most likely dead and he could be dead in a minute too. His martial arts training instinctively kicked in and he calmed down sufficiently to stop the pounding of his heart. He moved cautiously, eyes darting everywhere till he got back to where the other was crouching in the near pitch black of the night.

Thankfully, it was a moonless night and even the stars seemed to have gone into hiding. He quickly told them what he had just heard and his suspicions that their colleagues had been killed. His plan was to go back to the headman's house where they had kept most of their equipment, and then bury their colleagues quickly if indeed they were dead before heading away from the village.

He told them to follow him in formation, spread out with eyes and ears open. The sense of danger was high, and they knew without a doubt that their stay in Yemowei village was over.

Jide felt the chills wash over him again as he recalled how close they had all come to being slaughtered that night. He was almost at the headman's house when he heard what sounded like an urgent whisper. He had frozen immediately and started counting how many seconds he had left to live when he heard the whisper again. It was a female voice, warning him that he was stepping into danger and begging him not to shoot.

She garbled an explanation that she had been hiding close to the house when the men came and hat, they had made away with everything they had left in the house except for the stuff they had hidden in the ceiling. They had also left two men there to take them out the minute they stepped in. Jide did not know what to believe.

The story, coming from the whispers in the dark, sounded incredible but she knew about the stuff in the ceiling! How had she known about that? As if she could read his thoughts, she said she had been in the house the day they came but had chosen to keep away because she was also on a clandestine mission herself. If fact, she had been in the very room where they had hidden the things; her uncle knowing that she would not want to be seen had told her to stand behind his big old wardrobe.

Jide recalled now that the old man had insisted on following him into the room and had warned him that he was not to open the wardrobe because that was where he kept his fetish items. How stupid of him to have believed! The room had been very dark, and he had suspected nothing.

All this explanation had come out in a few minutes

and the girl had slowly come of her hiding place behind the plantain trees with her hands raised. They were about halfway to the head man's house, and she advised that they return to where they had left the others and move a way from the village immediately. She had been trembling with fear as she told him she was a journalist and would explain why she was in Yemowei. But they needed to leave.

They had left, running cautiously into the bush around the village and in the direction of the footpath that his men had been guarding uselessly. They were only a few metres away when they met Soje, gesturing frantically for them to go back. His partner had been hacked to death a few minutes earlier and his saving grace had been the fact that he was in the bush relieving himself. He had overheard him telling his killers just before he died that they would find his other colleagues asleep in the headman's house. That had been a ploy to alert Soje in the bush so he could run back and warn the others.

All that had been over a week ago. And now here they were: three men down and one girl with a British accent and a raging fever, climbing trees and being shot at in the middle of nowhere!

Jide and his men had accepted the girl's story and she had proved to be as brave as could be expected in those circumstances.

But no one was being brave now. They were all frightened and fatigued.

10

They moved a little further inland and the leader of their small group called for a rest. They sank gratefully to the ground, leaning against various trees for support. Jide was still tense from the action of a short while ago. He was not quite sure what to think; had the militants been shooting at them? If they were, how come they had come no closer? His reverie was interrupted by the leader.

"Make una try to sleep small because the next place wey we go pass, bad well well o!" We no go fit waka for night, and if you no shine eye, na one time pesin go die troway!"

Jide was dismayed by what he had just heard.

The man had said they needed to rest up for the next leg of their journey which would be more dangerous than anywhere else they had been so far.

That was not good news at all. He wondered if this mission would end with them all dead. His thoughts wandered to his mother and what she would be doing. Very likely she was spending endless hours on her knees, praying to her God to keep him safe. He had often teased her that she prayed too much, and she would reply calmly that here was nothing like too much prayer.

"But Mom, did you people not tell us that God knows everything and owns everything? If He knows so much, why do you still need to keep praying to Him all the time?

"Are you not my son? Why do you still ask me before you take my things for your use?" His Mother would retort? And they would go back and forth. Their arguments about the existence of God had no end, and sometimes Jide deliberately started the argument just to tease her. She knew that of course, but she would still take time to explain. He smiled to himself in the dark. His mother, he hoped to make it out alive for her sake. He could not imagine how she would take the news of his death.

His thoughts were interrupted by the voice of their 'leader' as he had begun to think of the man helping them to escape.

"Wetin all of una dey come find for dis place sef? Una talk say we no good; gofment don tif we land finish. Oyel don spoil all river, no fish again and no food. People dey die and pikin dem don turn to ashawo and tif tif. Una come carry gun come dey fight we people. Wetin una dey find? Untili we die finish comot for dis place una no go rest!"

Jide was in shock. He could not believe what he had just heard. The man was grumbling about their presence in the region and complaining that the government had stolen all their lands and rendered them homeless and practically income-less because the land had been destroyed by oil spills. The young people had turned to prostitution and armed robbery, yet they were being killed.

Jide did not know what to say, or if he should even say anything, but the man was not done yet. He continued in his dialect and from the way his voice rose and fell in the sing-song way that Jide had come to know, it was clear the man was trying to control his anger.

The man spoke for long minutes with the occasional grunt from his partners. Learning bits and pieces of the Ijaw language had been part of their training for this mission but none of them had really taken it seriously and Jide did not know more than a few words and phrases. But this man was not even speaking in the main language. He was speaking in a dialect that sounded similar but was obviously different and he could not pick out the meaning of anything he was saying. But it was obvious the man was angry, though he tried to keep his voice down. He wondered if this was the end of the mission right here; the man sounded angry enough to finish them off right there.

Suddenly, they heard Alero responding angrily; at least it had to be Alero because she was the only female in the group, but Jide could not believe what he was hearing. She spoke in the man's dialect and to Jide's ears, albeit untrained, she sounded like she spoke the language perfectly.

She was talking in the same, slightly raised, quarrelsome tone and he could not make out even one word of what she was saying. They both continued for a long time obviously arguing about something and it sounded like they were both angry with no one willing to back down. As they continued, Jide felt his own anger rising. Along with the anger he felt a mixture of shame and disgust.

He felt ashamed of how easily he had fallen for Alero's good looks and perfect demeanour, and he felt disgusted with himself for believing her little story about being a journalist in search of a story. What a fool he had been! And now he was about to find out how much of an idiot he was. This girl was clearly one of 'them' whoever that was. Before he could say anything, he heard Soje speak up angrily.

"Miss Alero, please could you explain to us how come you are conversing with this man in his local language? Did you not tell us you are a UK based journalist? Where did a UK based journalist with such strong British accent and a name like Alero learn the language of the creeks and become so fluent in it?" Is your name even Alero? Please tell us the truth for once, even if you and your people plan to kill us in this jungle. At least we should know who our killers are, out of courtesy."

It was clear that Jide and his men were thinking the same thing. Soje sounded angry, but he also sounded resigned to the possibility of betrayal and death.

Alero and the man continued to argue back and forth in fierce whispers. She did not as much as speak a word of English by chance. The other man soon joined them and after a few sentences, Alero finally spoke in English. "Don't tell me that please!" she said in obvious anger. Jide and his colleagues were still in the dark and it was clear whose side she was on.

"Chai!"

Gbaja made the one-word sound that could mean surprise and disgust and a myriad of other things depending on usage. Timmy was quiet. But that was usual, he never spoke if he did not have to. But Jide had to say something.

"Alero, please, what exactly is going on here?" She was quiet for a few seconds during which every sound in the jungle was amplified because of the tense silence. Then she began to speak.

"Our hosts seem to think that everyone else is to blame for their problems except themselves. They blame the government, the media, the oil exploration firms and even the international community; but they refuse to accept any responsibility for the situation in which they find themselves." They are as much to blame as anyone else for the devastation of the Niger Delta region!"

"That still does not explain how come you are speaking the local dialect with such fluency, Alero. That is the explanation we all are waiting to hear from you. Who are you? Don't you think we deserve to know the real you by now?"

11

"My name is AleroYenimiere Oyinkuro. Everyone calls me Alero Kuro. Alero is the name given to me by my Itsekiri Mom at birth. My father legally changed our last name to Kuro, shortly after I was born. My Dad is from Yemowei but I had never visited the place until a few months ago. The story of my life and how I came to be in Yemowei at this time is one you may find interesting, but it is a rather long one."

"Please, go on, there is nothing else to watch on TV." Soje was obviously being sarcastic, but he had made his point and Alero continued.

"My father was one of the beneficiaries of the Federal Government special scholarship for indigenes of Yemowei. He was among the first set of people to travel to Britain from Yemowei on scholarship. He was a stellar student, and the entire community was very proud of him. As a scholarship student, he did not have money for frequent travel. So, he rarely came home but kept in touch with his people back home. He was an orphan, raised by his maternal uncle whom he regarded as his father.

"My father worked during the holidays, saving up as much of his money as he could in anticipation of his return home. Then in his final year he met and fell in love with my mother. She was in her third year in the same university, and they met in the library. It was love at first sight for both of them."

Alero paused, as if she was contemplating how much of the story to tell. No one said anything and she continued after a few minutes.

"My Dad knew immediately that he had found the woman he was going to marry but he did not have the guts to tell her right away. But he did ask her contacts. They kept in touch and within a few weeks it became obvious to all their friends that these two were in love. But there was a problem which they both knew. The Ijaws and the Itsekiris were tribal enemies. And while my Mum's family were liberal people who could allow their daughter to follow her heart, my Dad's family was more narrow-minded.

"When they heard about his relationship with an Itsekiri lady they threatened to disown him if he did not end the relationship. He refused to end it and they made good on the threat. They disowned him and even wrote to the scholarship board that he was no longer representing the community. His tuition for his final year was already paid so he was able to finish.

"He was offered a job immediately by the University library. He married my Mum in a quiet ceremony and enrolled for his Masters' degree programme. By the time I was born, they were both settled in England and doing relatively well but my father missed his home. He missed his people and from the things he read in the news he knew that trouble was brewing in the region.

"He wrote long letters to several newspapers under his new name, warning of the dangers of taking the resources from the land without developing the region. He was mostly ignored but he kept on writing. To keep his memories of home alive he started teaching my Mum his dialect. And then he started to write down every word; he made sure we only spoke our local dialect or Ijaw language in the home.

"By the time I was three years old, I could speak my three local languages as well as English. By age six I could read as well as write all four languages. By the time I left high school, I had become a polyglot. I spoke French, German, Spanish, Itsekiri, Ijaw and, of course, English language. Then my father made me learn Yoruba language as well. By this time, he had produced a dictionary and several other books.

"From my earliest years I knew I would be a writer. I wrote for my campus magazine and several other publications while I was in school. It was easy getting a job and with my language skills I have travelled extensively in Europe writing and interviewing people. I was particularly interested in minority issues, I hold a Masters' degree in Indigenous studies, and I am currently working on my Ph.D.

"My father was forced to become an armchair activist, but he planted the love for the people and the land in my brother and me. And he always told me I would go back home some day and make a difference where he could not. He died two years ago and when this opportunity came for this assignment, it did not take long to convince my Editor that I was the right person for the job.

The village head of Yemowei is a distant cousin of my father's and he was the only one who stayed in touch all these years. I knew I would be welcome in his home for as long as I desired, and I also knew he would keep my identity a secret like I wanted.

"We were getting deep into the history of Yemowei when he was notified of your coming. And as it appears, the militants also knew you were coming. The betrayal very likely came from the village though, but as they say, the rest is history."

12

Jide could not believe his eyes. They were standing at the edge of a large expanse of swampy land that stretched as far as he could see. There were some strange looking trees spread across the expanse as if someone had deliberately arranged them there. He could not recall ever hearing or reading about any place so strange in his life and he dreaded what he was about to hear.

Alero and the man seemed to have come to some sort of truce after her long story and he had urged them to sleep a bit before dawn. But sleep had been impossible for Jide. His mind was filled with the things he had heard from Alero and from the man who grudgingly told them to call him 'Aboy.' Aboy had concluded his grumbling last night by declaring that there was no God. And if there had ever been in the past, he had surely left long ago and gone on to more favourable lands. His concluding words spoken in almost perfect English haunted Jide the rest of the night. He had simply declared: "God is not here."

And now here they were standing at the edge of a marshland that seemed to lend credence to that claim. Aboy gathered them round for final instructions. They were indeed going to cross the seeming endless expanse of land and it was important they did exactly as they were told. They were to walk in single file with him leading and one of his friends bringing up the rear behind Jide. He would be followed by Alero and Soje with Timmy behind Soje and before the second of the men, then Gbaja Jide would follow.

They were to keep their eyes in front and place their hands on the shoulder of the person in front; one wrong step and the entire train go plunging into the deep swamp and would end up in the belly of a happy crocodile. Even Jide was shaken at the thought of the crocodiles, and he could see Timmy had his eyes shut in prayer. Even he looked unsure, although no one looked as frightened as Soje.

Aboy tried to reassure them that if they followed him closely no harm would come to anybody. He had done the crossing before and though it was always harrowing, it was indeed possible to get through. The advantage was that no one ever came this way. Tofumando had a deep fear of crocodiles. It was rumoured that the only woman he ever loved had been eaten alive by a crocodile long ago and ever since then he avoided them as much as was possible.

They set out at as the sky was lightening over the horizon. Aboy had stressed the importance of setting out early in the day. The crocodiles would have been well fed in the night and would be less likely to attack the humans foolish enough to venture into its territory. It was not a story that offered a lot of confidence, but they had no choice but to set out all the same.

They were so quiet that they could actually hear each other breathing. They moved at a cautious but reasonably fast pace, careful to hold on to the person in front and follow closely but carefully. They had been making steady progress and had moved for a little over two hours in silence when Jide noticed that the sky looked overcast, and he found himself praying silently that it would not rain.

He did not know what the consequences of rain would be in this dangerous wasteland. They were passing through a portion of the terrain that had more trees than usual and he did not relish the thought of being soaked in addition to being frightened. But as if to punish him for daring to pray, the rain began to fall. And immediately Aboy gestured to them to climb into the trees nearest to them.

They scrambled up as quickly as they could, and the last man had barely pulled his legs up from the ground when a giant crocodile pulled out from some reeds a few feet from the tree and slid into the swamp a few feet away! Jide could not believe how close they had come to being devoured.

For the next two hours they were forced to cling to trees like monkeys as the rain pelted down with a vengeance. It was not supposed to be rainy season, but in the Niger Delta, the rain was as unpredictable as the English weather. And it stopped as abruptly as it had begun. But Aboy called out to them to remain in their uncomfortable perch for a while longer. They were cold, hungry, and tired but the sight of the crocodiles slithering in and out of the muddy water a few feet away was enough to keep everyone alert.

They waited for another hour before he decided it was safe for them to move. They could see a few of the beasts on the other bank of the swampland and it looked like they had all gone over to that side for some reason. But just as they were about to start climbing down, the ground very close to the tree Alero was on moved suddenly.

A beast so big and so well buried it had seemed like a part of the ground raised its snout and the ground literally shifted. She let out an involuntary scream and it seemed like every crocodile and every creeping beast for miles around responded in a frenzy. They moved and heaved and slithered all over the place. There was no question of going anywhere now.

They were stuck up in the trees for as long as it took for the animals to settle if they ever would. "E be like say na top of this tree we go sleep today." The man was stating the obvious and no one wanted to say anything. There was no need to argue anyway. Everyone tried to climb even higher up the trees and look for comfortable positions. It was difficult.

The biggest fear they had to deal with was tree snakes. If snakes appeared on any of the trees the only option would be the ravenous crocodiles below. Talk about being between the devil and the deep blue Sea. The situation they were in was much worse. A sense of gloom began to descend on the group, but Aboy would not let them hold a pity party.

He began to speak, loud enough for them all to hear but in even tones that sounded non-threatening. Crocodiles had very good hearing and he did not want to agitate them any further. "E get one time like dat when me and my friend dem dey cross this place. We no quick comot and rain come dey fall like dis. Crocodile dem full everywhere; n so my we begin waka on top of the big crocodile dem and notin hapun to us."

Jide did not know if he was trying to be funny or if his story was true; either way he was not amused. How was it possible that he and his friends had walked on the back of these dangerous animals and made it out alive? He would not even ask for an explanation. The story was too incredible to be true.

"I know say una de tink say I talk lie but na true." He was quiet for a while after that when no one responded to him. The men were all lost in thought and Alero was sniffing up in her tree. Jide wished he was on the same tree with her so he could comfort her some, but she was on Gbaja's tree and there was no going back and forth in the foreseeable future for any of them. The owners of the territory were still prancing around below.

Dusk soon crept in and he wondered what they would do in the night when sleep crept up on them.

As if Aboy was reading his mind, he spoke up a bit louder than the last time.

"Make enibodi no try to sleep oh. If you sleep and you fall comot for your tree na die be dat one straight. Crocodile no dey sori for person and you no go fit run for dis place." Make I tell una one tori." And with that he launched into the history of the land.

When the man began to speak all thoughts of sleep fled from their eyes. He was a walking encyclopaedia of the history of the Ijaw people. He told of how his people originally came from East and Central Africa and finally settled in the Niger Delta. He traced their ancestry through the Ife dynasty and the Binis. He regaled them with stories of their exploits, some ignoble during the slave trade.

As he spoke, he broke into soft singing and illustrated his history lesson with anecdotes from a time before the devastation of the land. Alero seemed to be the most intrigued of them all for obvious reasons. The man spoke almost nonstop for several hours. And Jide wondered how one, so seemingly illiterate could be so vast in history and so eloquent in presentation.

Although he spoke in his usual pidgin English, he reeled off dates and figures as if he were reading from a book. If Jide had not been right there, perched high on a tree, next to the man he would not have believed what he was hearing. The bizarre nature of their classroom for this history lesson made it all the more interesting.

Between Aboy's history lesson and the vicious bugs, they were kept awake all through the night. The mosquitoes sang and feasted on these human intruders all night long. They feasted as if they could not believe their luck and by morning, Jide and his little group had swellings all over their face, hands and every exposed part of the body. While the history lesson had been going on up in the tree, the beasts below had been hunting and feasting on whatever it was crocodiles fed on in the swamps. Jide assumed it was fish and he wondered how any fish survived the endless attacks. As the day dawned brighter, the storyteller told them to get ready to climb down and continue their journey.

He whispered to them to maintain the quiet and to increase the pace. He did not need to say it twice. They quickly found their places in the human train and began moving once more. They moved much faster this time. The threat of the beasts around them, the harrowing night they had just endured, and the danger that they still faced, made them forget all thoughts of personal discomfort. Soon the trees became closer together and the ground firmer underfoot. They were nearing the end of the marshland and they increased their pace even more. They passed by a small pool of clean-looking water and before anyone could stop him, Soje bent down and scooped a handful and drank greedily.

"Soje don't!" they all shouted in unison, but it was too late. He had taken as much as his hands could carry. They were all going crazy with hunger and thirst, but they also knew that the water in the creeks was not safe for drinking. "Make una leave am. Belle go pain am small but we don nearly reach where we dey go." Jide did not even have the energy to reprimand the young soldier; it was obvious the young man was past caring what happened to him.

Finally, they came out of a thickly wooded area and found themselves on a cassava farm. They were safe! They had crossed the terrible crocodile territory and come out safe on the other side.

"Make we jus' move small reach that side before we rest."

None of them spoke in response to Aboy's suggestions that they move a little further before they took a break. The men just grunted and Alero made a sound that was more of a whimper than anything else.

At last, he moved into a little clearing between some trees and gestured for them to sit. They all collapsed to the ground in gratitude. Jide looked at his wristwatch and saw that it was almost 4pm. They had been on the move for almost ten hours!

And it had taken them almost thirty hours to cross the land of the crocodiles. Aboy brought out something that looked like smoked meat of some sort and passed it around. They all took it silently. Too tired to do anything more than mutter a few words of gratitude. Alero was still whimpering in one corner and the others all seemed to be in various stages of despair, but it was clear they were all relieved to be out of the immediate danger the crocodiles had represented.

"Oya, make we try to sleep small before day go dark. I know this area well well. We go fit move for night tili we near Trofani."

With that, he lay on the grass and was soon snoring. But Jide could not sleep though he was just as tired as the rest of them. He lay on the grass, staring up at the canopy of the trees. "Boss, do you think we will get out of here alive?" it was the first time Gbaja had said anything in several days and Jide turned and faced him in the dim light. He had to remind himself that these were young boys, though well-trained.

"Gbaja, I believe that we will not lose any more men on this mission. We have come so far that I believe the worst of it is over. As soon as we get to Patani, we can make contact with HQ for pickup. I am sorry I have not been the leader I should have been." Jide had never been more sincere in his life and he felt like drawing the younger man close to himself.

"Boss, you have been an exceptional leader. Your strength and focus in the midst of all this has given me the courage to continue. And to say the truth, I now see you as my big brother. If you had not kept your cool, we would all have been long dead!"

Jide did not want to argue. He knew he was no hero, but he felt warmed by the young soldier's words. He must have fallen asleep because next thing he knew he was being shaken awake by Aboy. He was naturally a light sleeper, and he felt a little upset that he had needed to be woken up. He looked around and saw that the others were still asleep except for Timmy.

"I slept too Boss, but I've been awake for about a half hour. And don't worry, I was the one who told him to wake you up. He needs to get us something to eat, and I know you will want to be awake when he leaves here."

"Thank you, Timmy. How's that hand holding up?"

"Pretty well, all things considered. It could have been worse."

They both kept quiet for a minute as their minds went back to their colleagues who had been killed in Yemowei and the harrowing events of the past couple of weeks. They knew their lives had been changed forever.

13

Aboy soon returned with a handful of his 'harvest.' He set about gathering sticks and soon had a small fire going, using a cigarette lighter which Jide recognised as his. It must have been taken off him when they were captured or rescued a few days earlier. Soon, the man was roasting sweet potatoes as they moved closer to the fire.

It was not a cold evening. In fact, it was quite warm and very humid but there was something very appealing about the warmth of the fire. The others woke and drew near to the fire. Aboy brought out a Swiss Army knife which Jide knew must also have been a 'war bounty' and cut the potatoes in halves and handed round. Food never tasted so good! They ate with relish, but could only eat so much because there was no water to drink.

"For night we go enter Trofani go find water. Trofani people dey do festival but I be egbesu and I no dey fear." Jide and his team had heard about the dreaded egbesu cult during their training. It was many of the cults that operated in the area, and if the rumours about them were to be believed, they were fearless and untouchable.

No wonder Aboy had ventured into crocodile territory the way he did. The Egbesu cult members were believed to have supernatural powers so long as they adhered to the requirements of the cult, whatever those were. "Boss, I think you may have been right about that water. I don't feel too good." Soje sounded like he was in a lot of discomfort, and he looked terrible too. Before anyone could ask how he was feeling, he started throwing up violently. Then he crawled quickly into the thicket beside him and from the sound and awful smell that hit shortly after, he was in major trouble.

"Oya, make we dey go. We no go fit treat that im belle if we no get beta water."

The group stood up wearily. They had hoped to rest for a little while longer, but Soje's condition would not allow it. They had barely moved fifty metres when he again ran into the side of the footpath to repeat what he had done earlier. He came out panting and sweating. Now they had another sick person besides Alero and Timmy to worry about. And from the look of things, they could lose Soje very quickly if something was not done soon.

Aboy and his men conferred briefly, and then two of the men stood on either side of the sick Soldier and practically carried him and moved off swiftly. They moved at a very fast pace. Jide and Gbaja soon did the same with Alero who was beginning to lag behind. Aboy led the group, and this time, Timmy brought up the rear.

Soon they began to hear sounds of humanity activity. The smell of cooking and the voices of children playing floated in the air. They had reached Trofani at last. Jide was both relieved and apprehensive. Relieved because Soje had made two more toilet stops and he was practically being carried now. Apprehensive because Jide did not know what awaited them. He no longer feared betrayal from these men but who knew what they would meet in Trofani village?

A few metres from the edge of town, Aboy gestured for them to hide in the bushes while he sent one of his men to go for help. As soon as the man went out of sight, he gestured for them to move away from where the man had left them. he told

Alero in their language that if the man was ambushed, they would have the benefit of seeing any attackers before he led them to where he had left the group. It was a wise move, although it did nothing to instil confidence in them.

Soje had emptied the contents of his stomach, but he was still heaving and squeezing. If he did not get medical attention soon, he would die before their eyes. Jide did not relish the thought of losing another of his men. He began to pray to the God in whom he did not believe. He knew that Timmy was praying too, and even Alero was muttering under her breath.

How ironic! Jide was praying to his mother's God in a land where the people believed that God Almighty, if He existed, could not be found. They had spent two weeks traipsing through a land so devastated by petroleum exploration that the only place where there was a resemblance of abundant aquatic life was a crocodile-infested jungle that was inaccessible to any but the most foolhardy and desperate of all men.

As they had travelled through the creeks and bushes Jide had been faced with the evidence of the "curse of the Niger Delta; dead and dying plants and farmlands struggling to yield a miserable crop from a land that no longer had any nutrients to give.

Creeks and rivers shimmering with a film of oil that made sure there was no aquatic life beneath; a people so deprived that the very waters on which their lives depended had become the poison by which they died. And here he was praying, beside a man who had clearly said to him, "God is not here!"

Was God here? And if He was, would He hear, and answer?

14

It was another hour before the man came back. He was not alone, but from the tone of the conversation they heard from their hiding place, they were not in any immediate danger.

"Govment, do ee!" Aboy called out heartily in greeting.

"Ukoidou broda" the visitor responded then followed with a rapid exchange that was difficult to follow.

As they spoke Aboy gestured for them to pick up the almost lifeless Soje. His eyes were closed and his breathing shallow. The new man, whose name was Govment, had brought a bottle containing some concoction and he forced it between the lips of the young Soje, all the while chattering away with Aboy.

He did not seem overly worried at the condition of the young man before him. He kept pouring the liquid down his throat until the bottle was empty. After a few minutes Soje began to groan, his first sign of life in almost an hour. They heaved a sigh of relief and Aboy promptly stood up. He said something to Alero in their dialect and she turned to Jide and the Gbaja.

"He says we need to start going right away. We were supposed to spend some time in Trofani to recuperate but it is not safe. There's a faction here that is loyal to Tofumando and if they as much as learn that there are foreigners in town, our lives will be worth nothing in no time at all!"

They did not need convincing. The new man picked up Soje as if he was a rag doll and hung him over his shoulder and moved off. He moved at a surprising pace for a man carrying a full-grown adult. They almost had to run to keep up with him. The path was dark by now and they could not see a thing. Aboy and these men obviously knew the way and they made good progress. Jide soon lost track of time, but he was sure they had been on the move for close to an hour when the man stopped abruptly. He spoke very rapidly with a lot of gestures and Jide guessed he was giving them some sort of direction.

This time Alero did not explain. He slid Soje to the

ground and pulled another bottle from his pocket. He forced him to swallow the contents of the bottle and then handed over a third bottle to Aboy. He also handed over a small bag. He then shook hands with all the men and turned back. "Oya make we dey go. Trouble still plenty for this place."

They again carried Soje between Gbaja and Jide and went after Aboy. The going was more cautious this time, they were obviously very close to the edge of Trofani village and there was less cover from the vegetation. They could make out the shapes of houses and they heard the sounds of the villagers winding down for the night.

Jide's senses had been so dulled by the fatigue of the past few days that it took him a few seconds after Aboy called a halt for him to realize they were close to a very large River. He had guessed they were moving in the direction of the river, but he had no idea they were already so close. Aboy stooped down and motioned for them to do the same. He explained the plan in a whisper. They were to steal one of the canoes by the jetty and float it down river and then paddle it to Patani when they were well away from Trofani. It would not be easy, but they had no other choice.

The longer they remained in Trofani, the greater the likelihood of their being caught. Aboy explained to them that he would go with them up to Patani and then return to the creeks after handing them over to the military authorities.

They squatted at the edge of the River, and watched the activities going on around the jetty; fishermen coming from late fishing trips and others going out for the night.

Soon, all was quiet and Aboy and his silent assistant slipped noiselessly into the water. Without as much as a ripple, they untied and moved one of the canoes away from the rest and floated it closer to where the rest of the group were waiting. Gbaja and Jide carried Soje between them and Timmy and Alero came behind them very quickly.

They got Soje into the canoe with some difficulty but soon he was lying at the bottom with his head on Alero's folded legs. At first Aboy and his man rowed close to the edge of the river so as to not draw the attention of anyone watching from the village. But soon they were far away enough to row much closer to the middle of the river.

The current was high, but these men were born in these waters, and they knew just what to do. They passed other fisher men who were throwing nets into the river but refrained from calling out greetings to anyone; they did not wish to be noticed at all. They quickly passed Asaba Aseh in the distance and the lights of Patani town soon began to glow in the distance. No one spoke; they were too tense for banter and nothing about this mission was funny anymore.

At last, they were in Patani, and it began to look as if they had made it out of the jungle, but Jide would not relax until he was on the flight back to Lagos. They anchored the canoe by a jetty that was deserted and climbed wearily up the shore. The place was quiet, it was close to midnight and most of the town had gone to bed.

Aboy had promised to take them as far as the military barracks, but now he seemed reluctant. He was no longer as self-confident as he had been in the jungle. The jungle was his domain, but here he was literally a fish out of water and his discomfort was obvious. Jide understood.

The man was a rebel, and he could be arrested and held for questioning. He had fulfilled his promise to get them to Patani and if he did not wish to go any further, no one would blame him.

They stood there beside the road and waited respectfully for Aboy to take the decision to return to the creeks or risk taking them to the barracks. The latter won.

"Make we dey go. D barrack no far from here."

15

Soje was fully conscious now. Whatever the man gave him must have been some form of quick-acting antibiotic. He was still weak though and he slowed their progress considerably. Finally, Aboy and his man lent him their shoulders again and they moved faster.

As soon as the barracks came into view Aboy stopped.

"We go turn back for here. Dis soja boys go wan to make trouble if dem see we." Make una take dis boy go hospital quick quick oh! And make una tell d gofment make dem stop to dey kill awa people dem sake of this oyel. D oyel suppose be beta tin but we don spoil am."

He turned to Alero and spoke for a long while. She started to weep, gently at first but soon she was sobbing. Then he embraced her and shook hands with Gbaja and Soje. When he got to Timmy, he brought out a small package from the bag he had picked up in Trofani.

"Make you dey put dis merecin for the hand so dat e no go rotten." He hugged him very tightly and when he tried to speak it was clear that the hardened rebel had a lump in his throat. Jide felt terrible that he had nothing to express his gratitude.

"Is there any way we can at least contact you to show our gratitude for all you have done?" Do you have a child or any relative who would like to go to school anywhere in the world? You have done so much for us, we would like to do something in return, although there is really no way we can repay your kindness."

"Make you no worry about dat one." He pulled Jide close and whispered something in his ear. Make una dey go, na d gate of the barrack be dat."

They shook hands once more and moved off in the direction of the barracks. At the gate they were almost shot to death. Jide's request to see the commandant fell on deaf ears. He could not blame the soldiers manning the gates. These ere low-ranking men and Jide and his people were dirty, ragged and with no form of identification. Only the

Elsie O. Dennis

presence of the woman in their midst kept them from being killed immediately.

Instead, they were taken to the guardroom and locked up with three other people in a tiny cell. Alero was taken to another cell and Jide hoped she would be alright. He had no fears for himself; these were his people, and, in the morning, he would explain to the officer on duty. His only concern was for his men who were in need of urgent medical attention.

He need not have worried though. Gbaja and Timmy were asleep as soon as they found a spot to lean their backs on and Soje soon joined them. The cell must have felt like a palace compared to the places where they had taken shelter in the past few days! But Jide remained awake. The thoughts of all that had gone wrong in this mission ran through his mind.

He felt like he had aged a lifetime in a few days. He had learnt more in the past couple of weeks than he had in all his years in the military. He had been part of several missions before and he had always given a good account of himself, which explained his rapid promotion and the honour he had been given of heading this mission, but this time had been different. He had clearly underestimated the 'enemy" this time.

He had dealt with different kinds of enemies and fought in various wars internationally, but this time the enemy was different. This time, the two fronts had the same enemy, but they were fighting themselves.

He knew there would never be a winner.

Epilogue

Jide closed his eyes as the plane taxied for take-off. He knew that sleep would be impossible on this six-hour flight, and he did not mind. He had brought along a book he hoped to finish if he found the in-flight entertainment boring. But he knew he would be doing a lot of thinking and he suspected the book may not be opened, not on this trip anyway.

So much had happened in the past two months that he had barely had time to think. Escaping from Yemowei and getting safely back to Headquarters had finally convinced him that there was a God after all. As the plane climbed into the night sky, he deliberately allowed his mind to go back to that night in the barracks cell at Patani.

The commandant had eventually sent for him by 7am, and though he had wanted all the details of the mission, Jide had insisted on telling him just enough to get the man to call headquarters. Apparently, they had been given up for dead when they did not check in for so many days. Their GPS signal had been lost and there was no way of tracing them. Searching for them had been almost futile, but a search had been initiated all the same. It had been fruitless, and they had given up when the signal came from Patani that they had been found. Headquarters had immediately sent a helicopter to Patani to pick them up and them to Port Harcourt from where they had been flown to Headquarters for debriefing. By the time they got to the headquarters, it became clear that they were in no condition for a proper debriefing. They needed urgent medical attention.

They were in the military hospital for three weeks before they were certified well enough to go home. All, except for Soje who was being treated for extreme paranoia in the psychiatric unit.

Timmy's hand had obviously been saved by whatever it was the rebels had applied in the jungle, but he still needed a lot of attention. The wound was now healing nicely and there was talk of a prosthetic hand so he could function normally. His days as a combatant were clearly over though. The rest of them had been treated for malaria and various other infections they did not even realize they had.

Operation Yemowei.

What a disaster it had turned out to be! Two men dead in the creeks. One on the verge of insanity and another home, without one hand. Gbaja was giving serious thought to getting married to his high school sweetheart when he recovered. And him, what had he come away with? He allowed his mind to wander.

He had come away convinced of the futility of the fight the government was fighting in the creeks. The approach was wrong. In his notes he had made his point clear and hoped someone would listen to his viewpoint. His boss had laughed at him when they discussed the issue.

"Jide, let me tell you, the problem of the Niger Delta is too complex for you to understand after a few weeks in the creeks."

Jide had restrained himself from arguing with his boss, but he knew the man was wrong. The issues were complex, but the solution did not need to be so complex. He had seen these people up close. He had listened to them and observed them in their own environment. They were a people yearning to be understood and treated right. For decades they had been exploited and misunderstood by various interests. The oil companies had only been interested in profits. The government had been blinded by the relatively easy national revenue source the oil represented, and the community leaders had been carried away by the handouts they got from the oil companies and corrupt government officials.

Everyone had won for a time, except the real owners of the land. The fishermen and the farmers had lost their source of livelihood; the land had been destroyed forever, and the young people had lost their dreams even before they had the chance to understand what it means to dream. It was a bad situation, but he didn't think it was hopeless. In his debriefing notes, he had mentioned the urgent need for all stakeholders need to sit down and agree on a position that would be acceptable to everyone; a position that would see the region developed, the land preserved, and the heritage of the people protected. He did not think it was an impossible task if there was a willingness to do what was necessary. Whether or not his recommendations would be taken seriously remains to be seen. It was completely out of his hands now.

He shifted his thoughts to the real reason for this trip to the UK. He had told everyone he was going on a well-deserved vacation, but he had another plan. He was actually going to woo Alero and convince her to marry him. She had refused any medical treatment when they left Patani and had insisted on leaving on the first available flight to the UK. However, they had spoken almost every day since then. The more they talked the more they found they needed to talk about. They spent countless hours on the phone, and he felt he knew more about Alero right now than he did about anyone else on Earth. And he wanted to spend a lifetime learning more!

As he cleared customs a few hours later, war and peace in Yemowei was very far from his mind; all he could think of was how to win the heart of the woman he knew he could not live without, no matter what else lay in his future. He smiled a nervous smile.

Acknowledgements

This book lived in my spirit for a very long time as I watched the events unfolding in the Niger Delta region of Nigeria, Africa's most populous country. I am grateful to my husband of many years for encouraging me to keep writing. His support has been the biggest boost for this and every book I have written.

I am grateful to my son, Brumeh, my first fruit who takes his time to read my work and spot the errors that I miss. To my other kids, I'm grateful for accepting and applauding my decision to live the life of a full-time writer in these turbulent climes.

I have been greatly helped by God, through men and women too many to name. I am indebted to all the people who make my writing life possible. Special thanks to my dear friend Pastor Tokunbo

Emmanuel, who at great personal cost, took on the task of preparing this edition. Thank you, dear friend and brother.

To God Almighty, the giver of life, without whom I am nothing, I say, Thank You!

Other books by Elsie O. Dennis

1. Twilight at Dawn
2. Gold River
3. Warri Chronicles
4. Clarity versus Reality
5. Management
6. Nuggets From the King of kings
7. The Speaking Donkey and Other Stories
8. Animal Naming Ceremony
9. Animal Naming Ceremony for Junior Readers
10. Tales My Mama Told Me 1&2
11. Lessons from Noah's Ark
12. Midnight Essays
13. Help! My Teenager is an Alien
14. What Bola Taught me About Friendship
15. One Night in Jibia
16. One Christmas Morning
17. The Vaccination
18. Sons of God, Daughters of Men
19. Ikumena– You Can Have That Baby